Daryl Cobb lives
children. Daryl's writing b
jor at Virginia Commonwea
writing class inspiring a
combined with his love f
music and the guitar, he discovered a passion for song-
writing. This talent would
motivate him for years to
come and the rhythm he created with his music also found
its way into the bedtime sto-
ries he later created for his
children. The story "Boy on
the Hill," about a boy who
turns the clouds into animals,
was his first bedtime story/
song and was inspired by
his son and an infatuation
with the shapes of clouds.

Through the years his son and
daughter have inspired so much of his work, including "Daniel
Dinosaur" and
"Daddy Did I Ever Say? I Love You, Love You, Every Day."

Daryl spends a lot of his time these days visiting schools
promoting literacy with his interac-
tive educational assemblies "Teach-
ing Through Creative Arts." These
performance programs teach children
about the writing and creative process
and allow Daryl to do what he feels is
most important -- inspire children to
read and write. He also performs at
benefits and libraries with his "Music
& Storytime" shows.

Manuela Pentangelo lives in Busnago, Italy, near Milan, with
her flowers, family and friends. She was born in Holland, but has lived
all of her life in Italy. A student of
architectural design, Manuela
discovered that her dreams and
goals lay elsewhere. She likes
to say that she was born with a
pencil in her hand, but it took
a while before she realized that
her path was to illustrate for
children. Manuela often vis-
its London, where she likes to
sketch at the British Museum,
and likes traveling to differ-
ent places to find inspiration.

She is a member of the SCBWI.

Printed in the USA
10to2childrensbooks.com

Pirate Words

ahoy - a word used to hail a ship or
a person or to attract attention.

crow's nest - a small platform, near the top of a mast,
where a lookout has a better view when
watching for ships or for land.

sea legs - the ability to balance yourself to the motion
of a ship, especially in rough seas.

poop deck - the highest deck at the stern of a large ship,
usually above the captain's quarters.

marooned - stuck someplace, usually on a deserted
island, with no way off.

yo-ho-ho - no literal meaning, but an exclamation associated with
pirates.

matey - a way to address someone in a cheerful fashion.

weigh anchor - to pull the anchor up and leave port.

avast - a command meaning stop.

Blimey! - an exclamation of surprise.

doubloon - a Spanish gold coin.

hands - the crew of a ship.

lad - a way to address a younger male.

lass - a way to address a younger female.

pillage - to steal something by force.

port - a seaport; a location where ships dock.

scallywag - a villainous or mischievous person.

swab - to clean, specifically the deck of a ship.

scurvy - mean and contemptible.

Arr! - an exclamation.

buccaneer - a pirate.

ye - you.

aye - yes.

$A+$

Pirate Firestone

Pirates:

Written by
Daryl K. Cobb

Illustrated by
Manuela Pentangelo

Do Pirates Go To Forest Brook Elementary School?

10 To 2 Children's Books

Written by Daryl K. Cobb
Illustrated by Manuela Pentangelo

10 To 2 Children's Books

Time to Read

™

To the students at Forest Brook Elementary School.
No one knows what the future has in store for them
so don't be afraid to follow your dreams!

Daryl K. Cobb

To Daryl, my parents and to all the little pirates
that are out there dreaming.

Manuela Pentangelo

Pete was running down the street.
He had some very happy feet.

He found a pair of pirate boots
someone had thrown away.
He couldn't wait to try them on.
It was the perfect day to play.

Pete went right
up to his room
and with no one
else around,

he slipped the boots
onto his feet,

"Now, come on boy, it's over there.
Lad, you need some pirate hair."

"It's the biggest ship, docked in the bay." That is what he heard Paul say.

On the sign, letters in bold, read, "Forest Brook Pirate School 68 Years Old."

Pirate Cipri & Ricker's Class

Pirate Club

Clarkin	Guerriero
Classey	J. Kelly
Conroy	Bombard
Floegel	Kessler
Garvey	

First Mates

MacDonald
Mulligan
Rivera
Woolsey

Pirate Talk 101 is the first class of the day, and 'aye' is the first word that I want to hear you say."

"Aye!"

"'Aye,' means yes. Now everyone, let's say it once again for fun."

"Aye!"

Paul then took out a list
of at least one hundred words.
For an hour straight they studied hard,
and not a single sound was heard.

Pirate Govits

Pirate E. Gatto

Pirate Fiorini

Pirate T. Gatto

Pirate Vogel

Behme & Scordo's Pirate Class

Pirate Brusca & Boehle's Class Was Here

"Avast," said Paul
"What does it mean?"
Peter took a guess,
"Stop, I think."
"You think?" said Paul,
"Aye," said Peter. "Yes!"

"Port,"

"pillage"

and "yo-ho-ho"
are all fine pirate words.

"Poopdeck"
prompted quite
a chuckle.

"Avast,"
the students heard.

"You all must learn to swab the deck
and hoist a sail or two.

Listen up, you scallywags,
or we may get marooned.

A crow's nest is not a place
for a bird to fall asleep.

A doubloon is the Spanish gold,
in the treasures
that we seek.

"Yo-ho-ho"
doesn't mean a thing,

but it sounds quite nice
when pirates sing.

"Ahoy" is how we say hello
to a fine English lass, and

"blimey"
is the word to use
when you are
late for class.

"Shiver me timbers" is what you say
in a state of complete surprise.
In other words, you say it mate,
when you can't believe your eyes.

Now it's Sword Fighting 101.
Remember, this is just for fun."

The first to try was Pirate Pete.
The crew all cheered and stomped their feet.

Peter moved with style and grace,
he flipped and leaped from place to place.

"Look out!" Paul heard someone say.
A rope had slipped, a mast gave way.

The mast and sail came crashing down,
knocking Peter to the ground.

"Peter, Peter are you okay?"
Peter answered, "Aye, Aye, Aye!"

Avast ye mates, I'm okay."
Then Peter kicked the sheet away.

His mom and dad were standing there,
a little bit confused,
when Peter jumped up from his bed
wearing ladies' shoes.

"Ahoy there, mates!" Peter said
with a yardstick in his hand.
"Pirate Pete is who I am!
You scallywags are on my land.

I hope you brought your sea legs, mates.
Weigh the anchor, set the sail.

We will be casting off right now,
to end this pirate tale."

Our dedicated crew also includes this scurvy bunch:

Ship Surgeon
Felice

Surgeon's Mate
Bento

Able Crew
Falco
Steinert
DiGangi
Braumann
Cruz
Godosis
LoVerde
Mroz
Saladino
Terracciano

Lookouts
Bragas
Divilio
Agnello
Lieberman

Pirate Lingo
Nicholls
Karszen
Boyce
Gustie

Pirate Art
Catapano
DeRosa

Deck Hands
Barnett
Fitzsimmons
Freijo
Giangarra
Gulotta
Lazzari
Manuel
Martins-Stephens
Punzone
Segal
Soldo
DeMaio
Sulinski
Wrenn
Beukelaer
Correia
Recinos-Archaga
Delaney
Noonan
Tsimis
Weil
Bibbee
Rae

Pirate Music
Deubel
Koehler

Pirate PE
Smith
Gutes

Forest Brook
Elementary School
2024   2025

*Join the adventure
and read!*

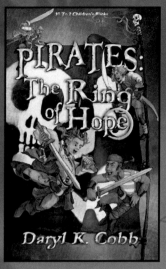
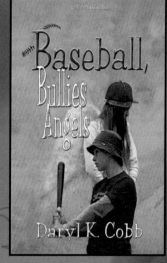

Made in United States
North Haven, CT
22 December 2024

62516764R00022